Mohammed Alfatih holds a Master's Degree in Accounting and Finance, loves reading and sailing in the world of imagination, was born in a beautiful era, and is a Sudanese national at heart and soul.

For all those who love reading, imagination, and diving into the worlds of beauty and creativity.

Dedicated to my father, mother, and brothers…my ultimate support in my life…

My soul is in my alienation; my dream is in my sleepover.

Also to you, my dear readers.

Mohammed Alfatih

DARKNESS OF KOZIEH

AUSTIN MACAULEY PUBLISHERS™
LONDON • CAMBRIDGE • NEW YORK • SHARJAH

Copyright © Mohammed Alfatih 2024

The right of Mohammed Alfatih to be identified as author of this work has been asserted by the author in accordance with Federal Law No. (7) of UAE, Year 2002, Concerning Copyrights and Neighboring Rights.

All rights reserved. No part of this publication may be reproduced, stored in a retrieval system, or transmitted in any form or by any means, electronic, mechanical, photocopying, recording, or otherwise, without the prior permission of the publishers.

Any person who commits any unauthorized act in relation to this publication may be liable to legal prosecution and civil claims for damages.

This is a work of fiction. Names, characters, businesses, places, events, locales, and incidents are either the products of the author's imagination or used in a fictitious manner. Any resemblance to actual persons, living or dead, or actual events is purely coincidental

The age group that matches the content of the books has been classified according to the age classification system issued by the Ministry of Culture and Youth.

ISBN – 9789948769743 – (Paperback)
ISBN – 9789948769750 – (E-Book)

Application Number: MC-10-01-3054707
Age Classification: 17+

Printer Name: iPrint Global Ltd
Printer Address: Witchford, England

First Published 2024
AUSTIN MACAULEY PUBLISHERS FZE
Sharjah Publishing City
P.O Box [519201]
Sharjah, UAE
www.austinmacauley.ae
+971 655 95 202

Table of Contents

Big Family	9
Squires	15
Aphid	21
Jara	28
Kozieh	43
Golden Coins	46
Treasure of Uncle Jacob	51
Battle of the Little Cliff	61
The Trial	72

Big Family

The beautiful village of Colmara, whose people were kind farmers working on the lands of the rich Squires.

At the end of each year, they harvested crops; half of which went to the owner of the land, and the other half went to the farmer. The farmer kept part of the crop for himself and his family, and the other part he exchanged for other things, and so on. Everyone lived in perfect harmony.

On a rainy night, full of lightning and thunder, Azura was running in the woods. He was the private royal guard, with two things in his hand; a letter and a necklace.

Azura was the father of the farmer, Chantelle. He was running, covered in blood, with a dagger in his back, holding onto the letter and the necklace, heading toward his house at the edge of the forest.

He opened the door, calling Chantelle, while everyone was asleep. His son came, and when he looked at his father, he ran toward him and grabbed him. He gave him the letter and the necklace and ordered him to bury them next to his house, whispering words to him.

The old man died that night, and his secret was with his son, who buried the letter and the necklace with his father in his grave by the cottage.

The next day, many royal guards and soldiers came looking for Azura. He told them that this was his grave and this was the dagger that killed him, claiming that he found it in the morning in the forest.

The soldiers left, and Chantelle returned, closing his door with his family to keep the secret with him.

In that year, a new king of the country was crowned with the blessing of the nobles. Many years passed, and Chantelle married, having many sons and daughters. The last of them was a little girl named Ashin, who was six years old, with blue eyes, and beloved by all the people of the village.

As for Chantelle, it was a name that had several meanings, including "the rocky land". Mostly, the reason for the name was because the family's agricultural lands were rocky and harsh.

Ashin was the youngest daughter of this family, and she had eight brothers and sisters, including four sisters and four sons, all of whom worked in agriculture to help their father in the fields.

Ashin stayed in the village with her mother and played with her friends who were the same age. She would return to her house, her mother would feed her and sleep next to her until her father and brothers came. They would wake her up from her sleep to play with her father and laugh with her brothers, and they would eat dinner.

She used to live her childhood days happily and warmly in the confines of her large family, feeling safe and not carrying worldly worries.

Ashin learned many languages from her hunter neighbor, who had traveled to many countries and met many people.

Three more years passed, and Ashin turned nine years old. She had mastered the art of sewing from her mother. Agriculture and farming did not appeal to her very much. Her father and brothers loved her very much and pampered her, allowing her to do whatever she wanted. From learning languages and sewing, she was elegant from a young age. She loved perfumes, sewed clothes, and spoke other languages in those dark ages characterized by violence, poverty, and lawlessness. The law was represented by the Squire, the owner of lands and palaces, and some guards, and also by the rich merchants who controlled the common people — the people of that time — who served as judges.

The Chantelle family leased more than eleven agricultural acres, which they had half of the annual crop from these lands. They were the only family in the region that had this abundance of land because their great-grandfather had been a faithful guard to the squire prince, whose name was Azura. At the end of his service after his death, the lands were entrusted to his son Chantelle, so he took over the task of cultivating these vast lands. As a reward for his father's devotion, half of the crop had to go back to the landowner in those days, and for many years, nothing changed.

Chantelle took advantage of this. Due to the vastness of the land and the abundance of crops, the family did not suffer from a shortage of food or money, unlike its destitute neighbors, who struggled annually to feed their families. The Chantelle family always extended a helping hand to them and helped everyone who was in the village, as well as their children.

Their neighbor Ezekiel and his son Armada were professional hunters, and they had no land. They became friends with the Chantelle family, and they all exchanged their fishing and crops with each other. They always spent very cold winter nights with each other by the fireplace.

Armada, despite his young age, was a skilled hunter and a close friend of Ashin's. He always brought her things from the forest. As for his father, Ezekiel, he used to teach Ashin many languages and read books and stories to her.

Their little girl, Ashin, lived in this atmosphere of love and respect from the villagers. She was like a princess in her clothes, her hair, and her eyes. She did not work in the fields, as her father and brothers took care of that. She used to create the most beautiful clothes and gifts for them and read stories to them on warm nights.

Until she reached her eighteenth year, a deadly disease, fever, afflicted the general population, and there was no treatment for it due to the scarcity of doctors, which made matters worse.

Ashin's mother died of fever that year, along with three of her siblings: two sisters and a little brother. It was a dark and gloomy year in Ashin's life. The burden on her father in cultivating the fields increased, and it became even more difficult because Ashin stayed at home alone.

This continued until Ashin turned nineteen years old, and she became the most beautiful girl in the village.

Ashin took care of household matters such as cooking, washing, and looking after her elderly father, as well as her brothers who worked in the fields.

Her two sisters got married and left the village with their husbands. Gradually, news of them ceased, as communication was quite challenging in the time of the squires.

Ashin grew increasingly lonely at home and set aside sewing amidst her many household duties. She reached her twentieth year.

The suitors came to her from the village and the neighboring villages, but she rejected them all. She was engrossed in novels and stories of love and lovers, and she was innocent, knowing little of the world beyond the walls of her house. The world at that time was cold, dark, and cruel, filled with blood, deception, hunger, and diseases.

She lived in what was known as the "Dark Ages", amidst hearts as dark as the rising sun. She resided in a house full of secrets and darkness, which she illuminated with her smile, like a jewel discovered by a pirate and hidden it between his ribs for fear of the treachery of time.

That smile disappeared with the passage of time, and she became preoccupied with household matters, taking care of her father and preparing food for her three brothers.

They lived together for a year without laughter or conversation. Armada brought her a book he had found neglected by the castle wall, hoping to bring back that smile.

She took it from his hands, and sadness covered her face. She used to read it to her mother and brothers, and this book brought back memories, so tears welled up in her eyes. They streamed down her cheeks and fell onto the pages of the book as she turned them. Armada did not know what to do; whether to wipe his hand on her cheeks or utter words to ease her pain. He could not do either, so he stepped back from her and left with his father on a new hunting trip.

The book was signed with the name Victoria. When her father and brothers returned, she set the book down and joined her small, now-grown family. Chantelle, her father, spoke to his children about the need to plant corn next year. He was optimistic about the land's production and hoped to save some money to make Ashin happy.

The three sons went to the village market, gathered the seeds, and stored them in the house until it was time to plant them.

At the end of that year, the collector came from the castle. Chantelle received him and delivered more than fifty sacks of rice, which was half of the crop. The collector wrote in his records that next year's crop would be corn.

The family was happy as the year passed, and they celebrated their harvested. They sold half of it in the market and kept the other half.

The preparations began with plowing and clearing the land, and with some money, they bought a huge buffalo to help with plowing.

They enjoyed happy days, helping their neighbors during the harsh winter days, and providing them with food. Ashin also sewed some woolen sweaters for the village children to protect them from the cold.

The village leader, responsible for it, ordered that the family be greeted every time they passed through the market. Ashin lived like a princess, thanks to the love and respect of the villagers for her and her family.

Squires

The village of Colmara belonged to the custody of the squire prince, Zekes. He was married and had two sons and a girl of Ashin's age named Victoria. She loved reading and politics and was interested in family affairs, as well as matters of trade and citizenship, unlike her two brothers. Prince Oliver was interested in hunting, battles, executions, and leading the soldiers in battles and equestrianism. As for his younger brother Jacob, he only cared about valuables such as shiny things, antiquities, and historical books. He spent most of his time in the palace library and prevented anyone from approaching his books or belongings.

A year after Ashin turned twenty, quarrels broke out between the squire lords. This was a common occurrence in those Dark Ages due to the absence of common law and the absence of a ruling class for the country. Each prince was the ruler and enactor of the laws of his own land and its inhabitants, and he was the implementer of these laws.

Zekes ordered the farmers to take up arms and go to his opponent's land to seize it by force, and the battle began. Leading this war was, of course, Prince Oliver, a hard-hearted and experienced warrior in matters of battle and the sword.

The battle lasted no more than twenty minutes because the fighters were not experienced in wielding weapons; they were farmers from both sides.

The farmers from Colmara village attacked the farmers of the other village in their fields, who had no idea what was going on.

The battle ended, and Oliver emerged victorious. The opponent's lands were seized, and their submission to him was declared. They now followed the squire lord Zekes.

Chantelle was wounded in the battle and returned home covered in blood, bleeding from his right leg. The doctor arrived after a full day and found the wound contaminated. He ordered the leg to be amputated to save the man's life, and that's what was done.

Ashin struggled with the care of her one-legged father, who couldn't adapt to his current situation after holding a position in the village. Now, he was left with one leg, unable to assist his children in the fields. No one visited him to ease his pain and loneliness. He could not go to the bathroom without help, and walking long distances left him tired.

His wrath unleashed on everyone he encountered, and he could no longer manage the work or tend to the fields.

He held a deep grudge against the nobles, despised the world around him, distanced himself from neighbors, and rarely left his house.

While his sons were eager to work, the vast land demanded constant care, and they could not afford hired help.

Land productivity declined, and debts grew. Chantelle could not bear the burden, and Ashin suffered with her father's mood swings. She began spending more time outside the house, tending to various needs and waiting for her brothers, who worked in the fields, leaving her father alone at home which deepened his depression.

One day, Ashin returned home earlier than usual. A friend had asked her to knit a woolen sweater for the winter. She opened the door slowly to avoid waking her father. She entered her room, gathered her sewing supplies, and selected a pink yarn. She then went to the living room, where she made a horrifying discovery: her father was hanging by his neck from a rope attached to the ceiling, with his favorite chair lying beside him, and one of his feet did not touch the ground, and the other was amputated.

Her father had committed suicide, a tragic moment for a man who had struggled throughout his life just to lead a simple existence.

In her confusion, she didn't know what to do. She ran towards her brothers with tears in her eyes. She eventually found them and broke the devastating news. They rushed back to the house, their hearts heavy with sorrow, and their legs moving swiftly, like horses in their speed. Together, they found their father's lifeless body, lowered it gently, and cut the rope from his neck. Ashin, overcome by grief like never before, embraced her father and wept loudly, her cries echoing throughout the village.

The entire community gathered at Chantelle's house, saddened by what had befallen this once-happy family. They wept alongside Ashin. She found a letter left by her father, instructing that he should be buried near his father's grave. In the letter, he described that the exact location where they should dig an additional five inches next to him and his father. There, they would discover a box intended for Ashin, as she was the only one capable of reading its contents.

The children followed the instructions in the letter. After burying their father, they retrieved the box to Ashin. She placed it in her room but did not open it. Her grief for her father had caused a profound shock that would affect her life and the life of her siblings forever.

It became unbearable for her to remain at home. She frequently went outside, sitting alone in the woods, waiting for her brothers to return, and they would come home together.

Armada noticed that she was always alone and sad, no longer smiling friend he once knew. This saddened him, and he tried to cheer her up by taking her hunting, but she no longer seemed to care about anyone.

Armada's father was seriously injured while hunting, and the village doctor was unable to save his life. Armada was left deeply disappointed, with no one left in the village to care for him. He felt betrayed by the forest that took his father's life.

Armada made up his mind to leave the village and go wherever his feet would take him. Perhaps he would find solace in hunting or someone to mend his broken heart, which he believed he had lost alongside Ashin and her sorrows.

The winter of that year was cold, and the dreary sound of music echoed from the castle, where some people were devoid of mercy and kindness. They laughed, danced, ate, and reveled in warmth, seemingly forgetting about the villagers and their hardships.

The regional princes and their king ranked among the richest squire lords in the country. Their wealth included vast farms, gold mines, abundant water sources and lakes, and forests teeming with various kinds of animals.

Their stables were filled with purebred horses, especially those belonging to Prince Oliver. He possessed a black horse that gleamed with its intense blackness, boasting thick hair, high and huge legs, and fast in galloping. He took great pride in this horse among the princes. During hunting trips, he personally cared for it and wouldn't allow the servants to touch it. In his last battle, he rode this horse and managed to defeat seven farmers without moving his sword. Oliver's sole interests revolved around warfare, battles, and his cherished dark horse.

As for the gentle Jacob, known for his elegant appearance, who genuinely cared about the servants and subjects around him. He could often be found in his palace library.

Twenty years ago, one evening, a young palace guard approached him to request assistance in writing a letter for him. Jacob complied with a smile, drafting the letter for the young guard. In a kind gesture, he even offer the guard some gold coins, which the hurried guard had unintentionally left behind.

Princess Victoria, the youngest of her siblings, was of Ashin's age. She always accompanied her father, Zekes, and took a keen interest in matters of governance, politics, and finance.

When she reached the age of twenty, her father entrusted her with the task of overseeing tax collection, managing the state treasury, and supervising the lands and the workforce in the gold mines.

"Golden Victoria" was her popular nickname among the public, because she was always seen amidst the golden mountains extracted from the mines or surrounded by gold coins in the palace treasury.

She showed no mercy to any of the workers or farmers who failed to meet their obligations or when there was a crop shortage at the end of the year. Her punishments ranged from imprisonment to flogging, or even selling them as slaves to merchants at the end of each year.

At the end of every year, she represented a nightmare for the villagers, not in black, but in the color of gold, known as Victoria. She spared no dignitaries or high-ranking merchants from paying taxes, and for those who were late in paying, she increased their debts until they could no longer afford to pay. Subsequently, she seized their assets, money, and lands, reducing them to mere laborers who often lost their homes as well.

Zikes, with the help of Victoria, became the richest man in the country. With Oliver's assistance, he also ensured his security. Even neighboring princes were afraid to disagree with him, and many chose to join his ranks, falling under his command. Consequently, the village of Colmara grew poorer, while the palaces grew richer.

As for Jacob, he grew increasingly isolated within his library, distancing himself from conspiracies, murder, and deceit. He withdrew to protect his ears from the cries of hunger and the sound of whips inflicting pain on slaves throughout the land. The tenderness of his heart was broken by the looks of weakness and fear that he saw on the faces of his servants.

He isolated himself to avoid Victoria's power struggle, her greed, and hard-heartedness, as well as his brother Oliver, who sees the end of every matter in the edge of the sword.

Aphid

Winter had departed, taking with it the feelings of love and sympathy among the villagers. Now, everyone was preparing for the agricultural season.

The three brothers worked hard, plowing the fields, sowing seeds, watering the land, and monitoring the crop's growth. They sorely missed their father's guidance and advice, as he had been very knowledgeable about agricultural matters, never overlooking any detail. Consequently, every year, the Chantelle family reaped abundant harvests without the slightest loss from planting to harvesting. However, in Chantelle's absence, the three brothers encountered significant challenges during the cultivation process.

Throughout the day, Ashin would have her meal and then wait at the edge of the forest, eagerly anticipating her brothers' return from the fields so they could all go home together.

On a beautiful sunny day, while she was sitting quietly, a hunting dog mistakenly attacked her, biting her hand. Her blood flowed, and the dog's jaws were clamped onto her hand while she bled. She looked at him without blinking or screaming in pain, and the dog howled and growled.

Her gaze at the hunting dog was lifeless, robbed by time of her mother, her brothers, her father, mixed with the pain of the bite but without any anger toward the fearsome hunting dog that held her hand, tearing some of the bones of her left hand, amidst the flowing blood that reached the ground.

The dog became terrified of her calmness and those eyes. He quietly released her hand, sat down beside her, and made no sound. Ashin remained motionless.

Soon, the horses and their owners arrived, following the hunting dog, which belonged to Prince Oliver. All they found was a girl bleeding from her left hand, with the dog sitting beside her.

The Prince dismounted from his horse, along with some of his servants and companions, and approached Ashin with brisk steps. He grasped her bloody arm, examined her face, and found no tears or crying, only emptiness in her eyes.

His servants seized the dog, and he ordered his men to hurry to the palace, prepare a place for her, and summon the doctor.

He carried her in his arms, seated her on his black horse, mounted the horse, and galloped with it faster than lightning. The horse's hooves struck the ground like giant hammers as he held the girl in one hand and the horse's reins in the other.

Throughout the journey, Ashin remained silent until they arrived at the palace, a palace she had only seen from the outside throughout her life. The palace doors swung open, revealing guards, soldiers, and a long corridor in which the horse ran. There were two gardens on either side of it, each one more beautiful than the other.

They reached the palace's entrance, and servants helped her down from the horse. Two maids carried her to a room that had been specially furnished for her under Prince Oliver's command.

In her room, she found the doctor waiting. Memories of her father and the doctor from the day before rushed through her mind—thoughts of the wound's contamination and her father's amputation all flashed before her in mere seconds.

Her hand was promptly and expertly treated. The doctor called for her brothers to check on their sister, and they arrived without delay, feeling deeply honored and eager to learn about Ashin's well-being.

It was not known that Oliver, the hard-hearted, had any interest in the farmers. The servants and everyone were talking about that girl who had tamed the lion and captured the black-hearted Oliver.

News of the incident reached his father, sister, and brother, prompting them all to attend without exception. They were surprised by the calm demeanor of the girl despite the situation she was in. She did not speak to them but bowed out of respect and fear of these tyrants. She remained seated with her back to the window, the light casting a portrait of silence in their presence—the king and the prince.

Victoria paid no attention to her, assured that her hand was safe after the doctor's care, and left. After all, Ashin was from the common people and the working class.

Jacob returned to his books while she lingered in his thoughts. She stayed in the palace for three nights until her hand's wound had healed, then she returned to her humble home.

She was not very impressed with the palace and the servants, and Oliver never visited her again.

Her brothers had returned to tend to the crops as harvest season approached.

One day, they were awakened by a knock on their house's door, and it was one of their neighbors. Her older brother spoke to him briefly, then returned to sit among his brothers in silence. His two brothers urged him to get ready to go to the fields for the harvest. He did not answer them, but after several minutes, asked them to sit down; he had something to share with them.

They sat down, both shuddering and afraid of what might be said.

Their brother did not make them wait long, he said,

"There will be no harvest this year."

The younger brother shouted,

"Why? The crops look green and ready to be harvested!"

His older brother grabbed his hand and said,

"Sit down, and let's listen to our brother."

He continued,

"The crops may look green, but they are sick. They are infected with aphids, insects that eat the plant's stem from the inside, leaving it hollow and unsuitable for harvesting."

A year's worth of work had gone to waste, and they still owed half of the crop to the landowner, Prince Zekes. He was known for his unrelenting nature, showing no mercy to farmers who defaulted on payments. They could envision the stern face of golden Victoria, who might double their punishment by demanding more of the upcoming crop's yield or by selling and seizing their lands. If they didn't own the land, they would have nothing to settle their debts, and their sons or daughters might become indentured to her in exchange for their debt.

Ashin's family did not own the land; it was leased, and they did not have enough money to pay for half a year's crop.

There was sadness in the house, and silence prevailed. Throughout the day, no one spoke to the other or tried to find solutions. The situation seemed hopeless, and despair prevailed.

The following day, everyone awoke with sadness on their faces. Their farmer neighbor came over, and they all went to the fields trying to save what could be saved and harvest some of the crop, hoping to collect at least half of it to settle their debt with the landlord.

All the villagers pitched in to help the Chantelle family that day, marking the beginning of their final harvest.

With every passing hour, Ashin remained alone at home, uncertain of what her brothers were able to gather from the fields and whether there was any hope. Would they return with smiles on their faces or not? Would their land be confiscated, leading to their dispersal, or not? What would happen to her and her siblings? It was a day that felt like a thousand years.

The sun set, and the villagers returned home, utterly exhausted. They walked passed Ashin, but no one spoke because of their exhaustion. Ashin anxiously awaited her brothers, and her patience wore thin.

Then, she heard someone dismounting from a horse behind her. She turned and saw Prince Oliver approaching. Her heart sank, she could not move or speak as he took steps toward her.

It was over. The executor of the law had arrived, the hardhearted man himself. He firmly grasped her hand, displaying no gentleness in his dealings, especially with farmers. His words took the girl by surprise, leaving her unable to respond.

The Prince said,

"How is your right hand after the dog bite? Have you healed?"

He asked it with a terrifying smile, as he had never smiled in his life.

She pulled her hand away, and just nodded her head. He then mounted his horse and departed.

She couldn't believe what had happened; she thought it was the end. Someone was holding her hand, and she screamed:

"My hand is fine!"

She believed that he had returned again.

Her brothers burst into laughter.

"We know it is fine. Let's go home."

She prepared dinner for them, and with fear in her voice, she anxiously asked:

"Did you manage to get anything?"

Everyone laughed, and her brothers reassured her that they had harvested more than half of the crop, and that things were fine.

Ashin let out a sigh of relief, and smiled for the first time in years.

They all laughed together and enjoyed their dinner with some of their tired friends who had helped them in the fields that morning. They momentarily forgot about the looming hardships and reveled in their sense of accomplishment.

A month passed, and the gates of the castle swung open. The registrar left the governor's palace accompanied by horse-drawn carts with heavily armed guards. They visited every house and farm in the village, some of them paying money, some delivering their crops, and others fleeing, leaving their children and wives to face the collector registrar and his men.

As the sun dipped toward the horizon, the crowd arrived at the last house in the village. Ashin's brothers emerged, opened their warehouse, and took out sacks of corn. The registrar recorded the number of corn sacks, put the seal on the paper, and handed it to them, stating that the family had settled their debt. This paper bore the king's seal.

Darkness enveloped the village, but the Chantelle's home stood sturdy against the encroaching night. Ashin took out some salty meat, a gift from their neighbor, Armada, which she had kept in the shed. She cut it up, washed it, lit the pot, chopped up some vegetables, and made a hearty dish to celebrate the passing of the year.

She opened the door, called out to her neighbors and their children, and poured some soup for them with large pieces of meat in it.

In the days that followed, everyone returned to their own lands, and began cleaning the land for cultivation again.

Jara

Jara is an Indian name given to females, meaning "pink rocks". It is a new, unconventional, and rare name. The owner of the name Jara is characterized by a strong and feminine personality.

It was the name that Oliver used to give to that beauty who captured his heart, and he did not know her name—that blue-eyed girl with wounds on her left arm.

Oliver, the arrogant and powerful, the one with pride, prestige, and a strong-hearted, the brave knight, was afflicted with the disease of love. He tried to cure it many times but found no cure. He distanced himself from the one he loved, hoping that distance might help him forget his passion. However, he could not sleep. Whenever he closed his eyelids, she appeared in front of him with her hair, smiling at him in his dreams. She opened her arms for him, gazing at him with her eyes. He would wake up like a madman, while everyone else was asleep. He fought the battles as if he was defeated in wars. In that last battle, to save himself, he was overcome by passion and declared the victory of love, as he often did in such battles. He returned, captive to his heart, looking for someone who had become his slave.

Zekes knew his son well. He talked to him about that girl and the fact that he wanted to marry her. Zekes had no objection, even though the girl was from the common people. He loved his son and overlooked such matters. He ordered a meeting of the royal family. Jacob attended while carrying his book with him as usual, accompanied by Dalida, the keeper of his secrets, who was in charge of all the prince's affairs.

Everyone sat waiting for Victoria, who came in a hurry. Despite her young age, Victoria had the privilege of sitting next to her father, King Zekes.

The King ordered a banquet, and they all sat down to eat. Zekes sat at the head of the table, with Victoria on his left. The chair on his right remained empty, as no one dared to sit on it. Victoria sat next to Jacob, while Oliver sat at the far end of the table.

The King ordered everyone to leave, except for Dalida, who remained standing in her place. She was the sole exception among servants, soldiers, and high-ranking individuals allowed to attend.

King Zekes said,

"Prince Oliver is getting married, and I have agreed to the marriage."

Jacob welcomed the news, smiled at his brother, and wanted to leave. However, Zekes did not allow him to depart until he heard from Victoria.

Victoria replied,

"If the King had already approved, what weight does her opinion carry in this marriage?"

King Zekes responded,

"This bride is a commoner."

Dalida took a step back.

Jacob took a deep breath, turned to his brother, and offered a smile that did not reveal his teeth.

Victoria asked,

"Is she that village girl who arrived a few months ago with an injured hand and has three brothers?"

Oliver confirmed,

"Yes, she is."

A silence fell over the room for a few seconds, though for Oliver, it felt like years.

Victoria said,

"I don't mind if my brother is happy with her, but why is he marrying her? I can bring her to you as a slave and she will be at your command."

The table shook as Prince Oliver tightened his grip, warning Victoria against harming the girl. Victoria did not show any fear of Oliver's words. She asked permission to leave, but her father did not grant it a second time. He wanted to hear her answer, whether it was approval or rejection.

Jacob expressed that he had no objections and requested to leave, which was granted. He left with his maid, Dalida.

Victoria remained seated, facing Oliver, to tell him that she had no objections if he agreed to her condition.

Zekes smiled because he understood what was going on in his daughter's mind. Oliver was stunned by Victoria's condition. She gave him one day and one night. The father agreed, and the royal meeting ended.

That night, heavy rain fell, and Oliver sat in his room overlooking the palace gardens, watching raindrops falling down from the sides of his window in a beautiful view.

The village of Colmara couldn't bear such heavy rainfall, as it often lead to leaks in the roofs of the houses and damage to numerous farms.

That night, the villagers suffered hardship. No one could sleep, and the Ashin brothers rushed outside to inspect their fields after securing their roof. They left Ashin alone in the house.

She too went outside to check the barn and the bowls filled with that year's harvest, which had been knocked over by the mud and rushing water. She went behind the barn to fetch a bowl of clean water for washing when she returned.

After washing and drying herself, she went to her room looking for clean clothes. She found a green dress that she loved very much and tried to get it out of the closet. However, it seemed to be stuck on something. She took out all the things from the closet to find an old semi-open box that she had long forgotten.

When her brothers returned, they gathered around the fire to warm themselves. Ashin joined them and placed the box in between them. They brought an iron tool to open the lock and upon opening it, they found a beautifully decorated box unlike anything they had seen before.

They gathered around the opened box, with all four of their heads overlapping, looking inside the box to find a circular golden necklace. The lower half of the necklace represented the sun, while the upper half displayed a sailing ship. They were captivated by the beauty and luster of gold.

Their attention briefly shifted to a letter inside a smaller wooden box, sealed with red wax. However, since none of the brothers could read except for Ashin, They disregarded it and the three brothers returned their focus to the necklace, rejoicing in their newfound discovery.

Ashin entered her room to read the letter. It began by stating that the letter and the necklace were exact copies of those in the palace, prompting her to continue reading.

Outside, the brothers debated what to do with the necklace. Some suggested selling it in one of the major ports to a wealthy merchant or nobleman, in order to obtain a substantial sum of money that would help them in the rest of their lives, and to enjoy prosperity for a long time.

Suddenly, Ashin came out of her room in terror. She snatched the necklace from them and put it back in the box with the letter. Her brothers stared at her in bewilderment, and it was the eldest brother who finally spoke,

"What is in the letter?"

Ashin replied,

"Death and execution await us if the necklace and this letter come to light."

The youngest brother said,

"We were content with our simple life, so why do we need the necklace?" Another brother asked,

"Is there anything left from dinner? I'm still hungry."

The eldest brother fetched an axe to smash the box, then he used the wood for fuel to keep them warm.

As for the necklace, Ashin hid it in the barn after her brothers had gone to sleep, ensuring that no one would think about it again, especially considering the dazzling allure of gold.

Several days passed, and everyone forgot about it. The quietude persisted until a sudden knock at the door shattered their peaceful existence on the day when the brothers were taking their well-deserved rest. At the doorstep stood a royal envoy, bearing a summons from the royal palace that would forever disrupt their tranquility.

Oliver had agreed to Victoria's condition in exchange for marrying Ashin.

For that village girl, it was beyond her dreams to marry a prince who lived in a castle and ruled over lands, a brave knight feared by everyone.

Seconds did not pass before she remembered what was in the letter. She woke up from her rosy dreams, but what could she do? She couldn't refuse, as they were the ruling family, and in the world she lived in, beheadings were easier than picking roses.

Her brothers neither objected nor accepted, leaving the matter to her.

Ashin stood alone in front of King Zekes, who ordered her to marry Oliver. She had no right to refuse; it was an order from the King. She nodded in agreement, knowing the secret of the letter and the necklace.

Ashin married Oliver and lived with him for a year full of happiness, during which he helped her forget her old life. She lived the life of a princess in all its details, with servants, palaces, horse-drawn carts, guards to accompany her, and many cooks and tailors. Oliver loved her and softened his heart. He no longer went out much or robbed the poor shepherds, forgetting about ruling and battles, and leaving everything to his sister, Victoria.

Despite this, Ashin never forgot her grief, pain, and hatred for those who caused her father's death and the departure of her neighbor and friend, Armada.

As for Oliver, he made regular visits to his brother Jacob, as they were very close to each other. When he learned that

Ashin could read and knew many languages, Jacob liked her even more and opened his library to her. So, she would visit him sometimes when she was alone and Oliver was not in the city.

King Zekes took care of the Ashin brothers, and Victoria exempted them from taxes and land taxes, making their condition much easier.

Many months passed, and everyone was happy with the news of Ashin's pregnancy.

King Zexus, thrilled with the arrival of his grandson, ordered celebrations, provided food for the public, and distributed money to attendees.

The days of Ashin's pregnancy were difficult, and it was hard for her to move. She grew tired of sitting in her room or lying on her bed. She had read all the books given to her by Prince Jacob.

She called her maid to assist her and instructed her to go to Jacob's library. The library guard had orders to allow only Ashin to enter. He immediately opened the door for her. Ashin sat down, looking for something new to read. She spent some time resting in Prince Jacob's library.

She tilted her head to the top of the shelves and spotted a box that she had become familiar with not long ago. It looked exactly like the one she had seen before. Trembling in fear, she asked her maid to return to her room. She did not leave the bed that day, and her maid brought her dinner and some milk. She turned to her maid and asked,

"If I ordered you to do something, would you do it without telling anyone?"

The maid answered without hesitation,

"Yes."

Ashin ordered her to bring that box, describing its location, and the maid went to carry out the task.

Ashin waited for a long time, but her maid did not come back. She eventually fell asleep, and when she suddenly woke up, she began to search for her maid. The sun had already risen, and she removed the curtain from her window, inhaling the beautiful fragrance of the morning and watching the beautiful palace gardens with their high walls. Suddenly, her gaze was caught by a guard on the top of the wall. The guard was carrying the head of her maid, which he then threw over the castle wall before returning to his post.

She remained in her bed throughout that day. The door to her room received a gently knock, which, in her heart, sounded like the beating of war drums. In a loud and frightened voice, she responded,

"What do you want? Leave me in peace; I don't know anything."

A soft voice answered from behind the door,

"I'm your new maid, please grant me the permission to get in."

Ashin closed the window, drew the curtains, and allowed the maid to enter.

"Do you need anything, madam?" the maid asked.

Ashin replied,

"No, please stay outside."

Ashin kept her cool and did not show any reaction to the death of her previous maid, focusing on the well-being of her unborn child.

King Zekes invited his sons to a private family dinner, excluding nobles and servants. Jacob attended with his maid,

Dalida. Victoria was the first to arrive and whispered to her father. Oliver and his wife Ashin were the last to join.

They all gathered around the dinner table, talking, laughing, and enjoying their meal. Zekes reassured about his coming grandchild and wished the best to Ashin.

Everyone was about to leave. Dalida spoke to Ashin without introduction,

"What was your maid doing in Prince Jacob's private suite, searching his library, which was forbidden to all?"

Ashin paused, and Oliver turned to Dalida.

"What did you say to her?"

He grabbed Ashin by her hand, and they went out. He took her to her room, and then hurried back to his brother Jacob and asked him,

"What did your cursed maid whisper to my wife? Don't play your tricks on me, and tell me without equivocation."

Jacob asked,

"Do you know why I executed your wife's maid?"

Oliver replied,

"Have you gone crazy? How can you execute a maid I brought to my wife?"

Jacob calmed Oliver's anger, took him to his library, lowered the box from above the library, and opened it with a key which he kept tied to his wrist.

Jacob said,

"It seems that your wife knows our secret."

Oliver replied,

"It is impossible. How does she know? She is a commoner. Hey, do you still keep copies of everything? You always seek blackmail and games. If our father finds out that you still keep such a forbidden secret in our family, your punishment will be severe. Did he not order you to destroy the box and its contents, along with its twins?"

King Zekes entered the conversation, sitting in a corner of the library, which Oliver had failed to notice.

Zekes said,

"Let's leave this conversation until Ashin gives birth to our little prince. As for the twins in the box, we found them at the Ashin family's house, along with a letter and a copy of the necklace. Don't worry about your brother, Oliver; he tells me everything, and I know everything."

Then he directed his words to his son Oliver, "Do not fear for your wife; we will not do anything to her without your knowledge."

Oliver interrupted,

"Don't worry, father. If Ashin knows what is in the box, I will bring you her head in a box."

Jacob said,

"So, we agree that our rule of this country is linked to what is in the box, and I bet you that she knows about us."

***

Ashin, in her ninth month, agonized in her room, crying out, accompanied by the palace doctor and many servants, while the two princes waited outside. Victoria was impatiently waiting in the King's hall for the next-born grandchild of the King, whether male or female.

Zekes was in the cellar of the castle with his loyal guard, wielding a broken sword, that heartless fighter who refused to give up his rusty sword, broken at the ends. He compensated for its deficiencies with the strength of his body. Slow of speech, he only obeyed the King's commands and paid no heed to the orders of others.

Joy spread throughout the entire palace with the cries of the little girl. It was a girl. Fate once again smiled upon the golden Victoria; there was no rival for her even in the distant future.

The prince was delighted with the child, Jacob remained unresponsive, and Zekes was frustrated that his grandchild was a girl with no claim to the throne.

Zekes ordered everyone to leave and then returned to Ashin, without looking at the child, he said,

"What did you name the little girl?"

Oliver replied,

"I named her Kozieh."

Zekes headed towards Ashin and asked her, without any introductions, in the presence of Victoria and Oliver. Jacob rushed out when he saw the King's arrival, carrying the box, as he knew what his father wanted to do. Jacob entered one of the basements in the castle and disappeared.

"Have you seen such a box before?"

Ashin answered,

"Yes."

Victoria said,

"We will show you the contents of the box, but in the castle's basement. Can you come down with us?"

Ashin replied,

"Yes."

Oliver carried the child and brought her down, with Jacob returning to hold Ashin's hand, guiding her down the stairs while whispering audible words to her,

"Always to the left."

She did not understand anything. Everyone arrived at the prison cells inside the basement of the castle. The smell was foul, and the place was dark. Zekes lit one of the cells for her. Ashin approached and saw a skeleton chained to the wall. In another cell, three emaciated and weak-looking people were sleeping, one of whom appeared to be an old woman.

Ashin did not show any signs of interest, sadness, or exclamation, as Zekes was known throughout her village for his violence, fights, and injustice to farmers.

Everyone was astonished by Ashin's cold reaction to what she saw. They went to the next room, where the doctor was waiting. She carried the baby, who began to cry. Ashin attempted to breastfeed her for a while, but the doctor approached, gave her a bottle, and asked her to feed the baby with it. Everyone looked at her, reassuring her that it was a special medicine that helps to recover quickly.

Ashin brought the bottle up to her nose, and instantly recognized all the ingredients in the solution. She had assisted Armada's father in making medicines to carry on his travels, which gave her this knowledge.

She looked at Oliver and asked,

"Do I need to drink this?"

Oliver replied,

"Yes, of course."

With a knowing look, Ashin said,

"Yes, I know your nasty secret, you filthy monsters." She turned her gaze toward Oliver and said, "I loved you despite your evil, and I still love you despite your treachery."

Then Ashin rushed outside. Jacob laughed, and she followed her intuition, turning left to find an open iron door leading to an escape route. She ran, clutching her daughter in one arm while lifting her dress to run faster. The moonlight illuminated her path, leaving no place to hide. The voices of soldiers, guards, and hounds echoed behind her, but she did not care. Bleeding from childbirth, she ran to save her life and the future of her child. Tears streamed down her face, her heart filled with bitterness—the love of her life, her husband, and the father of her child, wanted to kill her.

Zekes ordered his guard that he wanted Ashin's head before sunrise, and Oliver rode his dark horse to rescue his daughter.

Jacob gave orders to Dalida after Ashin as well. Baby Kozieh cried loudly as her mother tried to calm her down, sitting by the river and leaning on a tree. The moonlight cast an eerie glow on the scene, mingling with the red blood that flowed from her. The little girl's cries persisted, and she had yet to be sated by her mother's milk. The voices of the soldiers drew nearer, and King Zekes' guard was the first to reach Ashin. He unsheathed his rusty sword and approached her, but Kozieh continued to cry, and Ashin remained motionless. He eventually stopped, lowered his sword, and took the crying child into his arms. Ashin did not move, weakened by the loss of blood from Kozieh's birth, the pain of betrayal, and the looming fear of what lay ahead.

Oliver arrived on the scene and found the little girl in the arms of that guard. He urged his horse forward, spurring it on with his legs, determined to rescue his daughter. King Zekes' guard, however, emerged from behind the tree and collided with Prince Oliver's horse, causing a chaotic tumble. Fortunately, Kozieh's small size spared her from harm as she was thrown and landed behind her mother's lifeless body, hidden from the turmoil.

Prince Oliver's leg was badly broken beneath his black horse, while King Zekes' guard emerged from the incident unharmed. The rest of the soldiers and Dalida arrived at the scene.

The King's guard, recovering quickly, approached to assist his injured prince. He extended his hand, but Oliver's black horse flinched, causing the guard to stumble and fall onto the prince. As the guard tried to get up, he searched for his sword and found it embedded in Oliver's chest.

Everyone was shocked. Blood flowed from Oliver's mouth and chest. Dalida, who had another mission assigned to her by Jacob, Turned her back to the gruesome scene.

She soon found the unconscious baby Kozieh, who was not making a sound. She swiftly picked up the child and disappeared into the forest, far from the prying eyes of the soldiers, who were shocked by the unexpected death of Prince Oliver.

Dalida raced through the woods, heading back to the palace to ensure the safety of little Kozieh. Along the way, she encountered an elderly man. Fearful of being detected, she hid herself until the blind old man passed by. His stumbling gait and frequent collisions with trees revealed his visual impairment.

Dalida gently took hold of the old man's hand, offering to accompany him out of the forest. He told her that on his way he stumbled upon a burning village and discovered the unconscious child. Believing she was deceased, he had intended to bury her.

The little girl remained unconscious from so much smoke, and the old man initially thought she was dead. She was an infant, a few weeks older than Kozieh. Dalida checked her condition as they walked out of the forest.

Eventually, the little girl regained consciousness, and the old man overjoyed, took her back. He thanked Dalida and assured her that he would take care of the child.

Exiting the forest, the old man mentioned his intention to visit Dalida as a way of thanking her. They bid each other farewell, and Dalida quickly returned to the palace, where she immediately went to the castle doctor.

Kozieh

After several hours, the soldiers returned to the palace carrying the two bodies and placed them in front of the king in the great hall. He removed the cover from his son Oliver's face, cried like a child, and ordered a royal funeral for him.

Victoria and Jacob stood behind the King, who ordered Ashin's return to her family in an old wooden box and then went to look for the child. Jacob approached him to inform him that she was fine and that she was in her room.

As for the guard responsible for Oliver's death, despite everyone testifying that it was an accident, his head was found hanging at the entrance of the palace, and his body was displayed on the palace wall with visible signs of torture.

Zekes quickly ascended the stairs, with Victoria, Jacob, and some servants behind him. He instructed them to call for the doctor.

The doctor appeared within moments, and Zekes whispered something in his ear, causing the doctor to visibly tremble. He entered Kozieh's room, and several minutes passed with no one moving from their places. Finally, a small cry emanated from the large room, a cry from an innocent child. Everyone waited anxiously. The doctor emerged with a small scroll soaked in blood, and the sight of it changed the expressions on everyone's faces. What had the doctor done?

He handed the scroll to the King, and as the king unrolled it, they saw the eyes of a little girl.

Victoria exclaimed,

"What have you done?"

Zekes replied,

"I did not want the girl to grow up, learn for the truth about the death of her parents, and look at me with those accusing eyes. So, I decided to let her live among us in darkness."

***

A blind old man carefully felt his way along a path, trying to reach the hut in which he lived next to some kind-hearted people. He carried a baby girl with him, not knowing how to care for her, He himself lived on some of his neighbors' aid in exchange for teaching their children martial arts and providing some advices to farmers regarding their cultivation.

He put the child next to him and fell asleep from the tiredness of the road. When he woke up, he reached out to check on the child but did not find her. He got up in a panic, and hastily searched for his stick to lean on as he got up.

His neighbor entered to reassure him that the child was with her, and she had breastfed her before letting her sleep. The old man sighed with relief, a smile returning to his face.

The neighbor inquired about the girl's name, to which the old man replied,

"The woman who saved her named her Kozieh."

Months passed, and the old man and his neighbor took care of the cheerful, happy, little girl with beautiful hair and blue eyes.

In the King's palace, Kozieh lived in darkness, seeing nothing and speaking very little. In the morning, servants were brought in to feed her and change her clothes, but in the evening, she had no one to play or talk with except for her maid, who took care of her.

Golden Coins

Two years had passed, and Zekes returned from his conquests only to find that Victoria had increased the gold mining operations and worked on the fertility of the agricultural lands. This, however, only made the slaves more miserable and the farmers more oppressed. She did not care for her citizens at all, and the name "Golden Victoria" had become synonymous with suffering, injustice, and cruelty. As a result, malice grew, and the farmers' hatred increased toward Zekes and his ruling family.

Jacob, on the other hand, had never cared about the ruling. He had traveled a lot, returning to the country only a few times and secluding himself in his library.

Fifteen years ago, Prince Jacob and his friend had been avid travelers, seeking to acquire precious things and listen to stories and tales. During their travels, they had come across a gypsy woman whose profession was traveling and singing. They sat in her company, paid for her services, and listened to some of the most beautiful singing and delicate instrumentals they had ever heard.

They stayed up all night, drinking a lot of wine, and she played the most beautiful melodies for them on a violin she had with her.

Jacob said,

"Give me this violin so I can play for you a little."

The gypsy replied,

"It is impossible for you; you will never touch that violin."

Jacob's friend said,

"Why? Don't you know who this man is? He is the prince of a kingdom."

The gypsy replied,

"Do you know whose violin this is?"

Jacob said,

"The gypsy will lose her head if she does not obey my orders."

The gypsy replied,

"You will lose your hands first. This violin belongs to Lucifer, the king of devils and the underworld. He made it with his own hands. He composed and played the presto of darkness on it. He has four prestos for four musical instruments, one of which is this violin, and the three are for the piano, the flute, and the harp found in the lost city of Atlantis."

Jacob said,

"Well, you don't need to give it to us; you play us that presto."

The gypsy replied,

"The presto is in my possession, and I will not play it as long as I live."

Jacob's friend asked,

"Why?"

The gypsy said,

"Whoever listens to this satanic presto will suffer a disaster."

"Moreover, this violin was made by the devil, and he played this presto on it, and everyone who listened to it was struck by a disaster or a curse."

Jacob was not scared; rather, he got even more excited to get that presto.

This was fifteen years ago.

***

Victoria owned several gold mines with thousands of workers and slaves. Thanks to her intelligence and her love for gold and money, the King's coffers flourished. She established a factory to convert the kingdom's gold into gold coins bearing the image of her father, Zekes. Those currencies were used in trade and all aspects of buying and selling in the kingdom.

Victoria's coins became official and widely accepted for transactions throughout the continent, making Zekes the master of feudal lords with his gold coins. Wherever he went, he was greeted by kings in their lands. All the nobles and princes borrowed from Victoria to solve their problems and manage the affairs of their kingdoms. Consequently, this Dark Continent bowed to Zekes and his family.

Zekes descended to the basement of his castle, a practice he often followed when overjoyed, to look at the third cell on the left bottom. There had been no sound from it for thirty years, and it contained three people and a skeleton.

***

The old man took care of young Kozieh, who was not yet ten years old. He taught her many books and languages, and she became his eyes when he traveled and when he needed assistance.

He could not do without her, and she never left his side. He served as both a father and a mother to her. They lived together in happiness, and her genius shone brightly. She developed a love for horses and horsemanship.

One day, Dalida arrived laden with gifts. The old man immediately recognized her by her voice, as she was the one who saved his little daughter from death in the forest that day.

Dalida gave him some gold coins for him and his daughter to spend. She left on her horse but was surprised to find Kozieh sitting on the horseback with her black hair and blue eyes.

Dalida helped her down and mounted the horse, setting off with Kozieh. They returned several days later, accompanied by a knight on horseback. This knight was commanded to teach Kozieh horse riding, and some martial arts that were not typically known by females at that time.

In Kozieh's heart, she saw bright days filled with care, love and kindness.

The castle palace was full of darkness and fear. Young Kozieh saw nothing but pitch darkness, silence, and isolation. Conspiracies and plots were being hatched next to her, and beneath her, a heavy oppression had been prevailed for years.

At fifteen years old, she knew nothing of the world beyond her room, her food and drink, the sound of birds in the morning, and the whispers of the servants in the evening.

None of the nobles approached her, for they had long forgotten her existence. Zekes, in his cruelty, feared having

Kozieh in his palace, with his dark secret hidden beneath the basement. He had no heir other than Victoria, and Jacob had his own goals far from the pursuit of power. Although others couldn't admit it, they were troubled by the prospect of a female ruler, as no woman had ever ruled a fiefdom. This matter disturbed Zekes's sleep.

One day, he awoke and realized that Jacob, his only remaining son after Oliver's death was missing.

He immediately went to Jacob's library, opened the door, entered the room, searched every corner, but found no trace of his son. He sat in Jacob's office chair, waiting for hours, until Jacob finally emerged through a secret door behind his desk, finding his father patiently waiting for him.

Jacob said,

"What brought the King of the country to my suite?"

Zekes replied,

"I would like to talk to you about a big matter."

He sought help from him so that he would rule after him and preserve the family's right to rule the kingdom.

He did not care much about what that evil old man said. He told him he was going on a trip, and when he came back, he would decide what to do.

Zekes said,

"Victoria seeks to rule the kingdom, and she put a condition before her brother Oliver in the past. If he wanted to marry Ashin, he would waive his right to rule to her. She seeks to rule all kingdoms and unify them into one country under her rule. The Victoria only thinks of gold and the rule and enslavement of people. She will ignite many wars and spend a lot of gold for that purpose."

Treasure of Uncle Jacob

Zekes left after that conversation. Jacob did not agree or refuse his father's offer; instead, he told him that he was going on a trip and would decide when he came back.

Jacob returned to his secret room beneath the library. There, he found an old chair with a red violin with black strings on it, scattered remnants of many bones, red blood staining the walls of the room, and a deformed dwarf cowering in the corner.

Fifteen years ago, in a dark cave, they had captured a monkey that had stolen a manuscript from the gypsy. Jacob and his friend had chased the monkey until they found it, and they had been elated by their discovery. They had found what they were forbidden to touch.

The gypsy had warned them against playing the presto and forbade them from doing so. Jacob had offered her a choice between a sword and money in exchange for the violin and the presto.

Jacob and his friend returned to their palace, indulging in alcohol along the way. His friend grabbed the violin and began to play it. Inside the violin was the manuscript containing the presto. As he started playing it, he did not even finish the first line before Jacob was overcome by excruciating pain, causing him to lose consciousness.

His friend, unable to release the instrument, continued to play. With each note, his body shrank by an inch until his eyes were nearly at the level of his toes, most of his body vanished, his face contorted, and he lost the ability to speak or move. He remained like this until morning.

Prince Jacob awoke to find a pool of blood amid the remnants of his friend, the violin still in his hand, and the presto lying nearby.

Fifteen years passed, and each time Jacob descended into his basement with someone to teach him the presto, he would lock himself in and be instructed to play the presto. He would start playing, and then the screams would begin.

He would wait an entire day before opening the door, only to find either a pile of bones or a mound of flesh, with the dwarf remaining unchanged, and the prince's will to live never returning.

***

Jacob set out on his journey as he had informed his father. Usually, no one accompanied him when he went out on these trips, despite being a prince with his own guards. He carried his baggage, mounted his horse, and set off.

About a month into his travels, he found himself stranded in a remote area, having lost his bag containing all his gold coins. He was left with nothing.

Eventually, he arrived at a tribe that lived next to a huge mountain that cast a deep shadow over it. The village sheikh and its people welcomed him, offering him a one-night stay before he would need to continue his journey.

They treated him to a hearty meal and showed him great hospitality, which pleased Jacob. They led him to a tent they had allocated for him to sleep.

As night descended, they cautioned him not to leave the tent, advised him to sleep early, and put a guard at the tent's entrance. The chief of the tribe entered and told him that today was a sacred day for them, marked by celebration and dance. Participation by outsiders was strictly forbidden.

Jacob paid little heed to these instructions, for he was a prince who was not used to being given orders.

As night descended, exhaustion overcame the prince, and he drifted off to sleep. However, he soon awoke with the urge to relieve himself. Outside his tent, he could hear the sounds of the tribal people, accompanied by drums, chants, and vigorous celebration. He pulled his head out of his tent to peek, in spite of the warnings of their chief. There was no sign of the guard. He found a great fire, around which the villagers were dancing enthusiastically. Men, women, children, and the elderly all joined in, accompanied by the beating of drums, their movements becoming increasingly frenzied.

It was not surprising, as he had encountered similar customs on his travels. He liked the movements of their legs in the dance, and as he lowered his eyes to observe more closely, he noticed tails emerging from their bodies, almost touching the ground as they danced. Horror and chills ran through his body, and he kept looking because he couldn't move.

The dancing got crazy, and they accelerated the pace. Suddenly, everyone fell silent. A frightening sound echoed from the top of the mountain, to which the villagers responded with joy, and they resumed their dancing.

Midnight approached. First, the children formed a circle near that fire, followed by the women, then the men, and finally, the elderly people.

The dancing never stopped, and everyone had their eyes on the mountain. Suddenly, a majestic winged creature with a hideous appearance descended upon them, landing amidst that the blazing fire. The people of the tribe rejoiced and got excited, with the drums and dancing intensifying. The creature joined their dance until dawn approached. With the sunrise, it spread its wings and flew back to the mountain.

As the sun rose, everyone returned to their usual state, and their tails disappeared. Jacob went back to his bed, terrified of what he had witnessed. He had hardly sat down when the sheikh of the tribe entered and asked him,

"Did you sleep well?"

Jacob replied,

"Yes, I have not slept like this in a long time."

Breakfast was prepared for him, and a beautiful woman served it, whispering,

"Have your breakfast and then leave. We know you didn't sleep last night."

Jacob was unable to answer her. She warned him to leave without looking back and cautioned that if he ever spoke of what he had seen, they would find him no matter where he went on this earth.

He did not touch the food, found his horse, and bid farewell to the kind people of the tribe.

He did not greet them. He rode his horse without looking back, and he did not go beyond a few meters outside the tribe's borders before his horse fell dead' most likely due to the horror he witnessed that night.

The prince walked on his feet for the first time in his life, covering a long distance until he reached the lands of the kingdom. The kingdom's guards recognized him immediately and brought a horse-drawn cart. Exhausted and tired, he sat in it.

He ordered them to hurry and return to the palace; it was a full day's journey passing through many villages.

The soldier obeyed Jacob's orders, using his whip on the horses' backs, causing the cart to move at excessive speed.

As they traveled, an old man came out from behind bushes, led by a young girl. The cart collided with the old man, causing the fifteen-year-old girl to jump. The old man trampled by the horses' hooves, and the cart passed over his torn body, killing him instantly.

The curtain of dust removed, and the cart stopped. Kozieh looked around, looking for the one who had been like a father and mother to her in this life. Instead, she found a torn body, clothes soaked in blood, and a face disfigured by numerous wounds.

She embraced her father, crying and screaming loudly, which drew the attention of the villagers who quickly gathered around. Jacob approached the corpse, utterly amazed at what he saw. It was Azura, the royal guard, who had miraculously survived to this day. He was the same Azura, who had fled on the night of the major battle in the royal palace, escaping with the secrets of the Zekes family. Azura was also the father of Chantelle, the Ashin family, and his brother's wife, Oliver. How could he be here after thirty long years?

Jacob, after having seen Azura's grave himself behind the Chantelle family's house on that fateful day, was now standing there with the soldiers. He ordered his soldiers to carry Azura's body and bring the girl in the cart.

***

They could not approach the corpse of the old man because the fierce girl, covered in dirt and wounds, would not let any of the soldiers approach her father, the man who had raised her.

Jacob turned to the villagers and asked,

"Who is this girl, and what is her relationship with this old man? He seems to know this old man's family very well."

The villagers explained that he showed up with her one day without warning, and he hadn't shared any information with them about where he had found her.

Jacob returned to his soldiers and ordered them to bring both the corpse and the girl to ride with him in the cart, as he had decided to provide her with shelter. His orders were swiftly carried out.

The girl managed to calm down, wiped her face, and combed her hair back, revealing her features. When Jacob saw her striking blue eyes, he asked for her name. She simply replied,

"Kozieh."

He laughed and then remarked,

"How can a common girl be called such an unconventional name?"

The girl, still grieving the old man's death, could not comprehend why this arrogant man was laughing.

He asked her again,

"What is your relationship with the old man? Don't you have a family or clan other than this old man to take you back to?"

Kozieh replied,

"He never spoke to me about who my family was, my father, or my mother. He was everything in my life, and I never needed anything he could not provide. I never felt the need to miss my parents or ask about them. However, there is a woman who has been visiting us continuously for the past thirteen years. She brings us money and gifts, and she has taught me many things."

Jacob asked,

"Do you know her name or where she lives?"

Kozieh replied,

"I don't know where she lives, but her name is Dalida."

"Ha ha ha ha ha ha!"

He burst into laughter. The only people around were his guard, his attendant, and his maid, all named Dalida.

He shouted at the top of his lungs,

"I will skin that Dalida alive when I find her." He turned to the little girl and said, "Do not worry, my little girl, we will find you a suitable shelter and someone to serve you. You are now under my personal care, and I am the prince of this country."

The cart had reached the royal palace. He got out of the cart, holding the hand of the girl Kozieh, and they headed to his private suite. In the corridors of the palace, they encountered Princess Kozieh. He stopped by her and greets her, and they exchanged greetings with him as he was the prince and her only uncle. He recommended his maid to take care of her. Then he returned to the other Kozieh, explaining that this little girl opposite her shared the same name, and was the little princess and granddaughter of King Zekes.

Little Kozieh immediately bowed, and the two Koziehs didn't exchange greetings. Jacob told her that she couldn't greet the blind princess because she had no eyes to see.

"Let's go." Jacob said.

Each Kozieh went in a different direction. One of them was a blind princess, and the other was a poor blue-eyed girl.

***

Jacob ordered the guards to summon Dalida. He sat in his room, while Kozieh did not know what to do. Jacob looked at her and called a maid who was standing near the door. He instructed her to take care of the child, provide her with clothes, food, and allocate a room for her after she takes a warm bath.

One of the soldiers entered, inquiring about what to do with the body they had brought with them.

Jacob replied,

"Place it in the basement until I inform the King."

Kozieh followed the maid, who helped her wash and change her clothes. They explored the palace together, and the staff brought her various kinds of food and sweets. When she sat on her bed, she couldn't help but notice how soft it was. She was not used to such luxury in life. She remembered those days with the old man in their little hut, enduring rain, feeling the cold breeze, and enjoying the summer air. During those nights, they had always held each other close, strengthening the bond between father and daughter.

Kozieh could not sleep, she was overcome with crying. She begged the maid that she wanted to see her father, the man who raised her, for one last time. Initially, the maid refused, but the girl's insistence made the maid agree on the condition that she could bid farewell to the man, and they would immediately return to their room without anyone noticing.

Kozieh, the blue-eyed fifteen-year-old girl, rejoiced.

In the middle of the night, the maid accompanied by Kozieh, crept around the palace down to the basement. They heard someone talking, so they hid quickly so that no one would see them. Kozieh peeped, witnessing Jacob in conversation with an old man. They waited until they were gone, then went on walking until they reached the basement. Kozieh asked,

"Who is the old man?"

The maid answered,

"He is the King of this country, don't you know him?"

Kozieh admitted,

"No, I did not know that this country had a ruler. My father always told me that the ruler was killed thirty years ago."

The maid chuckled, remarking,

"You common people only know how to compose stories and fables."

She opened the room in which the body of that old man was located, Kozieh sat next to him, and her tears fell successively as she hugged him tightly. The maid begged her to leave so that she would not be exposed and be punished.

Reluctantly, they exited the room, taking an alternate route to evade any potential witnesses. As they passed through the empty, dark cells with no life or guards, Kozieh was profoundly unsettled by a particular scene. She held the maid's hand tightly until she returned to her bed in the palace.

She slept that night with a tear on her cheek. The old man was buried in the presence of the King.

***

Kozieh Oliver Zekes woke up in her room as usual every day with nothing new, except for another girl of the same name sleeping next to her in the next room.

Battle of the Little Cliff

Nine days and one night passed, and Kozieh did not meet the other guest of the palace, Kozieh Jacob did not visit her again, as he had gone on another journey.

Kozieh went out for a walk in the palace gardens and enjoyed the unparalleled beauty. She glimpsed Victoria, adorned with golden carts covered in cloth, entering a tunnel under the palace. Curiosity led her to follow these horse-drawn carts. The guards did not notice her, as she was agile.

She sneaked behind the soldiers and entered a place resembling a cave, a gigantic chamber beneath the palace. Right in the center, the carts unloaded a vast amounts of decorated gold in the form of gold coins, piled on top of each other forming a small mountain that shone like the sun inside that dark cave.

Kozieh was mesmerized by the sheen and luster of these gold coins.

In past years, when Kozieh found one gold coin or when Dalida visited them and gave her three coins, she could live a month of bliss with the old man.

She recalled the simple people of her village, and how they suffered and struggled to get some money at the end of each month, or after selling crops, and the presence of tax collectors from palaces like this, who would take away what little the poor had, increasing their suffering and making them even poorer.

They returned to work as they were, only deepening their sadness over the passing days, accompanied by hunger and despair. This only fueled the darkness within them, mixed with hatred toward those who enjoyed life's blessings.

The soldiers finished unloading the carts and left. Victoria completed the money registration and also departed with the soldiers.

Kozieh sneaked around carefully, ensuring the soldiers would not see her. Eventually, she noticed a dark path at the end of the tunnel, leading from this cave of opulence to freedom.

She emerged from the cave, discovering an abyss and a small cliff overlooking some trees with a river flowing through them.

She sat there for a while, contemplating the scenery, waiting for the remaining soldiers to leave the cave so she could safely return to the palace without being noticed.

Kozieh navigated through the corridors of the palace in search of her savior, Dalida. When they finally met, Dalida was taken aback to see Kozieh in the palace. Kozieh ran and embraced Dalida, tears streaming down her face, explaining how the old man had died, and Prince Jacob had brought her to the palace.

Dalida, trembling with fear, grabbed Kozieh's hand and led her to Jacob's library. She advised Kozieh to escape and hide in any place where no one would recognize her. She handed Kozieh a bundle of money before hurrying away.

Dalida ran out, and Kozieh sat in the library, not knowing what to do. She wandered around, looking at all these books and artifacts that impressed her. As darkness fell, she made her decision and ran away from the palace.

Meanwhile, King Zekes inquired,

"Has Dalida returned from her mission?"

The guard replied,

"Yes, but she ran out again."

Zekes responded,

"It seems that she encountered Azura's child and ran away. Send golden Victoria's forces after her to bring her to me, no matter where she is. I want her alive at all costs because our fate is in her hands."

***

Nine days passed, and Jacob returned from his trip, only to hear the news that Dalida had fled the palace and that the soldiers were after her.

Kozieh descended from her room within the palace but could not find her maid. She became disoriented and ended up in the basement of the castle, where there were no guards in sight. She felt her way along the walls and softly called out,

"Is anyone there?"

There was no response at first, but then she felt a hand grasp hers, and the person on the other end chuckled like a child. Kozieh pulled her hand away in fear and asked,

"Guard, please take me back to my room."

He did not answer her, but the laughter continued, and another person joined in. Kozieh grew frustrated.

"Who are you? Do you both live in this palace? You surely can't be guards, so who are you? Why is this door closed to you? Who are you?" she demanded.

Someone called out from a distance,

"Princess, can you hear us? Where are you?"

Kozieh replied,

"Yes, I'm here."

The palace guards eventually located her and escorted her back to her room. She turned to her maid and inquired,

"Where did you find me?"

However, the maid remained silent.

Zekes advised Kozieh,

"Don't go out alone again."

Kozieh agreed, saying,

"Okay."

***

Our little Kozieh found refuge in one of the villages near the palace. There, she worked as a maid in an inn, in exchange for the accommodation and her food. She exuded cheerfulness and beauty, earning the affection of everyone. Her diligence in her work and her warm smile charmed all the guests.

Neither Zekes nor Jacob cared for her, as to them, she was merely a wayward girl who had been cared for by an old man who had since passed away. Consequently, they didn't send anyone to look for her.

One of the guests ordered food for himself and his friends in their room.

Kozieh brought the plates of food; they took them from her, gave her some money, and instructed her to close the door as she left.

She did as they asked her. She closed the door, and ventured into the corridor where she found some scattered items. She sat down and arranged them. Meanwhile, a conversation unfolded among the group inside the room,

"I overheard, by chance, about an order to assassinate the King." one of them said.

Without hesitation, Kozieh swiftly entered their room, her lips curling into a joyous smile. She closed the door behind her and whispered,

"I'm with you on this."

One of them unsheathed his dagger and headed toward her. His companion stopped him, inquiring,

"Did anyone else overheard our conversation?"

Kozieh replied firmly,

"No."

He asked her again after everyone had calmed down and reassured her,

"Why do you want to join us, knowing that failure could lead to death?"

Kozieh replied,

"I have faced death on numerous occasions. I spent a few nights within the palace. And then she told them her story."

The holder of the dagger replied to her,

"The death of the old man was an accident, and this does not justify you joining us. You bear a limited hatred towards a certain deed. But for us, we want to change the fate of our loved ones, friends, and everyone you have seen and lived with. Since Zekes took over this country, we have witnessed nothing but oppression of the weak and the execution of poor people. We live in perpetual darkness every night, and you have only experienced it for one night. You have not truly tasted the horror that comes when hope turns into despair."

Kozieh said,

"Zekes is not the ruler of the country."

Everyone fell silent, then murmured,

"What this girl is saying?"

Kozieh said,

"Give me a moment."

One of them got in her way to block her, asking,

"Where do you want to go?"

Kozieh replied,

"To my room to get you something. I don't mind if you come with me, and we will return together."

Indeed, Kozieh returned after a few minutes with a distinctive wooden box, and everyone in the room looked on. She opened the box, and a necklace and a message of it.

The holder of the dagger asked,

"What is this? A necklace? What do you mean? And a message? None of us is knowledgeable and knows how to read or write except for this friend of mine."

His friend took the letter and read it, then turned to Kozieh.

"Where did you find this?"

Kozieh replied,

"I found it in Prince Jacob's library in the King's palace."

The man said,

"You are our savior."

The men gathered their friends after devising a plan to attack the palace in the absence of Victoria and her golden guards, and with Jacob going out on his travels as usual. This way, Zekes would be alone in his palace among a crowd of soldiers who were not many in number.

***

Kozieh guided them to the small cliff, where inside there was a large cave below the palace, with several tunnels leading to the interior of the palace.

Everyone was ready and prepared, with Kozieh ahead of the crowd, for she had proven her ability to handle weapons. She was their guide to the royal palace.

After midnight, on a moonless night, they climbed the cliff and found a yard devoid of guards. At the end of the yard, they discovered a tunnel, just as Kozieh had described, leading to a cave filled with gold that left these simple people in awe. Their anger, hatred, and insistence on carrying out their mission increased.

The day before the mission was to be executed, Jacob left the palace and sent a message to Dalida, requesting a private meeting beneath the small cliff. Jacob and Dalida had been with each other for thirty years.

Dalida agreed to meet Jacob under the cliff of the castle. They met without soldiers or guards, just as Jacob had requested.

Before sunrise, the group heading for the palace had successfully scaled the cliff, leaving no one behind, as they knew it was an irreversible suicide mission.

Dalida stood with her hands behind her back. Jacob approached her hastily and shouted from a distance,

"How could you betray me, especially when you are the closest person to me? Haven't I not treated you like a princess and entrusted you with the secrets of the kingdom? Why did you betray us?"

Dalida replied,

"You are monsters in human form. You have killed, stolen, plundered, and oppressed the people. I know you're aware of Azura, the guardian of the kingdom, who fled the day you killed its king. You imprisoned his wife and infants under the palace a long time ago, and you took an illegal right to rule this country."

Jacob said,

"Your end is near."

He drew his sword, heading toward her in a fit of rage, intending to kill her.

Dalida, however, put her hands behind her back while holding a violin.

Jacob warned,

"Don't you dare do that!"

Dalida responded,

"For twenty years, I have been memorizing this presto of death so that we can hear it and die together."

Jacob ran towards her, but Dalida began to play her violin with the bow, causing blood to trickle from her blurry vision amidst the encroaching darkness. She was cursed. She continued until the end of that haunting melody. Slowly, she opened her eyes, finding Jacob with his sword thrust into her breast, whispering to her,

"I have heard this presto before, and there is nothing left for me to hear, you idiot. Die alone."

Jacob snatched the violin from her hands, and she fell dead under the small cliff, as bodies tumbled from the top of the cliff.

She closed her eyes, bidding farewell to our world for a darker one. Anyone who hears the presto would be cursed.

***

The crowd of hunters, farmers, and some powerful youth passed the hill of gold in the cave, guided by Kozieh.

Everyone found themselves amidst old, dark cells, and Kozieh stood there with the man who held the dagger, along with his friends from the inn, looking at the remnants of thirty-year-old injustices, now lying chained at their feet and around their necks.

The sight was incredibly frightening, and they did not struggle to open the prison doors, as they were rusty and worn out with the passage of time, much like the prisoners who had been inside.

They unchained them, clothed them in the garments they found with some other people, and carried them out of the palace through the tunnel leading down the small cliff.

The rest of the group returned to their original mission: assassinating the tyrant Zekes.

***

Kozieh and her companions crept into the corridors of the palace. A guard spotted them, but before he could react, the holder of the dagger skillfully killed him from a distance. This was his expertise in throwing daggers at festivals, and he turned to his friends with pride, indicating that he had saved them.

Ignoring him, they continued with Kozieh, who led them to the suite of Zekes. As soon as they opened the door, a barrage of arrows rained down on them, as a fully armored squad was stationed there to protect the King.

Many of the villagers were killed, and the survivors fled back to the cave to save their lives. The guards, soldiers, and Zekes himself pursued them.

Young Kozieh was struck by an arrow in her right shoulder, and the holder of the dagger picked her up and fled with her.

Everyone reached the small cliff outside the cave, but the soldiers were close behind them. Everyone took out their swords, preparing to fight for their lives. Their goal was in sight—freedom lay behind them in a cave filled with gold, and their hope rested on the possibility of a just ruler.

A fierce battle took place and continued until the sun rose, ultimately resulting in victory.

***

Hours later, Dalida opened her eyes and found herself amidst a pile of corpses. She wondered why she hadn't died despite the cursed violin and its devilish tune. Frightened, she fled and disappeared from sight.

Zekes, on the other hand, met his demise, struck by three daggers, a sword, and even a spear through his eye. The King was dead.

Those who survived celebrated, making the dawn of a new era.

***

The news of King Zekes' assassination quickly spread through the country. Victoria received the news while she was inside one of her gold mining mines.

Jacob, on the other hand, remained elusive and couldn't be found by anyone. As several days passed, nobles, sheikhs and rich people from the neighboring countries arrived in the nation to discuss the future governance of this country following the ruler's death, with the aim of preventing chaos.

Everyone gathered in the great hall of the palace, attended by those who had staged the coup against the ruler and were responsible for his demise.

The Trial

The hall was filled with the notables and opinion-holders of the country, including the esteemed de Rochelieu, the wise Intercastio, and the elder statesman among the merchants, Viscount Elmont, a recognized figure by all, seated prominently in the forefront.

Discussion began regarding the appointment of a new ruler for the country, along with the prosecution of those responsible for the coup against the former ruler and his subsequent assassination. All the attendees coveted Victoria's golden treasures.

One of the commoners in the audience requested the floor. It was not common practice for commoners to speak in the presence of the nobles and rulers of the country, but today was an exception. The guards were instructed to allow him to approach the center of the hall and address the assembly. He retrieved a letter from his pocket and began to read it. The document bore the seal of the country's ruler, was affixed below the letter on a golden necklace.

"Behold, Ugo Cabe, the true ruler of this land, along with his crown prince and brother, Ezekiel. We are the legitimate rulers of this country, bearing the seal of the golden necklace, a symbol of our rightful authority, endorsed by the elders and nobles of the neighboring countries. Noble Gasconier stands as our witness, his seal affixed alongside ours. We have designated our brother, Ezekiel, as the crown prince, and have decreed that succession shall pass to the eldest or most deserving among my sons or nephews.

"We have entrusted this letter to our chief guard, Zekes, to be its guardian and trustee."

Everyone was shocked after they verified the authenticity of the letter and the seal of the noble Gasconier, especially since his son, the noble de Rochelieu, was present at the council and bore the same seal.

A judgment was then issued that the murdered Zekes, his daughter Victoria, and his son Jacob had no right to rule the kingdom. Consequently, his granddaughter, Kozieh, was to be imprisoned, awaiting the consequences of her grandfather and father's deeds.

The focus of the assembly shifted toward the children of King Ugo Cabe. His wife and two sons were brought forward. She was asked to reveal the truth about the injustices that had befallen her family and to select one of her sons to rule the country.

She remained silent, having lost her ability to speak after thirty years of isolation from society.

The assembly turned their attention to the children, and the kingdom's chief physician examined them, revealing that they still possessed the children's minds and were unable to speak.

***

Chaos erupted in the great hall as it became evident that the king's sons were incapable of ruling, and many coveted the opportunity to become the guardians of the country because of the bounties it contains.

One of Ashin's brothers, named "De Winter" stepped forward to address the assembly. Everyone calmed down to hear what he had to say.

He stepped into the center of the hall and requested to see their niece, Kozieh, who was imprisoned with them, awaiting trial and most likely facing execution. He begged them, highlighting that she was blind and unable to see, and had suffered greatly in this palace. Everyone in the hall, both commoners and nobles, protested, viewing revenge against Zekes and his family, or what remained of it, as an essential and non-negotiable requirement.

Before returning to his seat, he caught sight of the golden necklace and requested to examine it up close. No one raised objections; they handed it over to him, and he examined it thoroughly.

De Winter spoke,

"I remember seeing this necklace tattooed on someone's arm a long time ago."

The leaders of the council read the letter again and posed a question,

"De Winter, was the man named Ezekiel?"

De Winter replied,

"Yes, he used to live next door to us, but he passed away a long time ago."

Frustration returned to everyone's faces.

De Winter continued,

"But he has a son about my age now, and his name is Armada."

Noble de Rochelieu asked him,

"Do you know where he lives?"

De Winter replied,

"Yes, he lives by the great river, and he is involved in hunting and occasionally trade. He is recognized for his huge body, and is loved by everyone there."

The order to urgently bring the so-called Armada was issued.

The council dissolved. Two days passed, and Kozieh languished in her prison. She could not determine which darkness was more oppressive: the darkness of her eyes, the hatred of those around her, or the darkness of her prison.

The council reconvened, with all members present. Armada was brought into the hall, where he faced questions about his family and origins.

Wise Intercastio declared,

"Bow before the ruler of the country, Armada."

***

Armada was crowned as the ruler of the country, and everyone was happy that the crisis had come to an end. They dispersed to judge the last tyrant from Zekes' family. They brought young Kozieh out of her prison, handcuffed. When King Armada laid eyes on her, he immediately ordered her restraints removed, moved by her pitiable condition. Everyone pressured him from nobles, sheikhs, and dignitaries to carry out her execution sentence.

However, Armada was unwilling to commence his first rule with the execution of a blind girl who had no understanding of what was happening around her.

De Winter and his brothers rose up to beg for Kozieh's life, offering to surrender all their lands in exchange for her pardon. They even offered that if she were forgiven, the public should not be burdened with her presence among them, and De Winter himself agreed to take her to another place.

***

King Armada was relieved by this resolution. He had been a close friend of Kozieh's mother and could not bring himself to order the execution of her daughter.

He issued the order to banish Kozieh and her aunts to a distant land, to expropriate their lands and return them to the state treasury.

***

Dalida reunited with Kozieh at the inn where she used to work, finding her with an injured shoulder.

With Zekes' rule now over, Dalida felt a sense of relief and chose to confide in Kozieh a secret she had kept for many years ago.

Dalida encountered Azura in the forest, each carrying a child. Azura was blind, so Dalida exchanged the children, taking the child from Azura and leaving Kozieh with the old man, who was blind and turned out to be her grandfather. The child who survived a house fire, also named Kozieh, found herself on the dark side of life.